UNDER NAKED SKIES

BOOK 2 OF

KISS THE SKY

BY

NIGIA STEPHENS

UNDER NAKED SKIES

Book 2 of Kiss the Sky

Copyright © 2017 Nigia Stephens

Published by Random Tangent Press

Print ISBN-13: 978-1-947957-01-5

eBook ISBN-13: 978-1-947957-0

Contents

UNDER NAKED SKIES

{1}

I sit naked on my man's balcony, my large blue wings fold back to catch the night breeze of New York City. Candles light our small table as he makes our evening meal. Jeremiah calls from the kitchen. "Nat, would you pour us something to drink? Do you like meat that's cooked all the way through or..."

"No, some blood is better, it means it was once vital, alive."

"Mmm, woman, the things you say sometimes gets me where I live!"

I laugh. I uncork the wine. Its rich cherry aroma wafts from the bottle as I pour our glasses.

I know, if our unfruitful, mixed-race union is discovered by my kind, I'd be made a Golgorn, an exile for spending any sexual heat with a human. Where I am from, it is illegal not to pleasure male nest-mates to bear young. If we are revealed, assets I've gained over hundreds of cycles and thousands of Earth-years will be confiscated, my command of Emera Cluster and my many victories in Blue Squadron will be stricken from our history. My people would do this to me as a cautionary tale to others.

It is modestly safer to commit to another female as a reason to refuse to breed with our males, but I've not found anyone that I adore in the manner I already feel growing for Jeremiah Gleason.

My gaze drifts to his comfortable living area, his books, his rustic leather-clad seating and to the wall of antique maps and old weaponry collected in his army days. Already, the faint but delicious smells of herbs and sounds of sizzling, drift in from his cooking. I feel a smile spread across my lips, I check my reflection. The short violet feathers of my head flutter in the breeze; my naked body, long dark limbs and oval face radiate a healthy glow from our pleasures. I am happy.

I think, Oh, the price we pay to follow our hearts.

I raise the glass and salute my joy before drinking. All that I am says this man's love is right for me. I want this to continue. There is nothing more I desire in my realm or in any other.

The air grows lush with roasted meats and caramelized root vegetables. Onions, I think.

He's singing along with a platter recording, then stops.

He calls out, "Nat, you ever heard this album before? Songs in the Key of Life? It's the first album I ever bought. There were CDs and MP3s back then but records sound better to me, fuller, real, you know? The singer is blind. He wrote all the songs too. Well, as far as I know."

I stop sipping my wine.

"Blind? There are not many crippled beings where I am from. We can cure most illnesses. Though, some are touched in the womb by curses and strange sciences from our enemies. They are born unable to fly, or worse, 'cause of these. It is spell-casting that is so old and powerful, it is beyond our ability to fix. Migdal's Scourge is an old curse of that kind. It kills little ones and the unborn."

I listen a moment longer. "His voice is rich. I like his singing very much but it's his words: They are beautiful to me, more poetic."

He says, "Mm-hmm. I thought you'd like him. He was a master of Soul in his time. Bet if his sight was cured at a young age, he'd never become Stevie Wonder, he'd never have developed the ear and voice for music."

I say, "You may be right."

Once more, he picks up singing in his soft baritone. The ease of conversation with him is like we've been together for years, but our first intimate encounter was just a night ago.

I take in more of the lovely wine and the warm evening air. Both my man's voice and this of Stevie, are lush and soft, much like how I feel at this moment.

I am a proud Oolran female, a Grandam. He thinks of me as one of our Earth representatives, a Valkyrie. I've fought in wars almost my entire life. I've battled for my people's existence and to protect the resources of our worlds. Never to defend my right to love whom I choose. I hope I never have to. This is all exciting and new to me. I look over my seat on his balcony, past my sanctuary, towering Riverside Church. I close my eyes.

I recall the details of the last battle of my command, the reason I was allowed leave off-world at this time, in my mind, I replay everything I remember.

Just beyond the devastated mountain regions of Graal, tens of thousands flee by air. Those that are born flightless, the very young and old and scores of others are in transports, we guard their passage. I'm bellowing orders at my cluster, the Emera. We sling spells and blast pulse rifles at our enemies, the air around us sizzles from the explosions of our net-grenades. The stench of the dead meshes with the sweaty fear smells of thousands as they flee. This time, it's the ore in our blood our enemies want. Captives are sucked dry for traces of life-giving micro-nutrients in our plasma.

The battle above the twin cities is as harsh as in the streets below. Down in the quads, we fight them as we fall back to the ground portals with more civilians. We muster every skill. We assault them with battle axes and swords, body cannons and blast shields, hands, feet and wings against mandibles and claws. Their parasitic host, Vis Stuvo, are the true enemy. We see their crews scramble behind their massive clear eyes.

A psi-order comes to my cluster from High Command of Blue Squad.

"Grandams of Emera and Alpac, peel off from transport lines. Take out the lead Death Bringer!" Two clusters, hundreds of flyers, descend on our enemy. We are impressive: segments of our filthy, silvery blue armor still glint in the strong sunlight. We form tight groupings, then dive and open fire with hundreds of body cannons.

I order, "Braincase and underbelly! Open 'em up, Emera!"

Alga, my second, spies a youngling recruit not in sync with the rest of us seasoned creatures. "Keep up, Rish!"

Rish is not slow, she just lags enough to be vaporized if she can't match our speeds in formation. Formation and precision is protection. It means a kill. It is what Emera Cluster is known for.

I hear chatter from familiar voices on my lively team.

"If she gets one of us killed, I'll blast her heart out myself!"

Another laughs, "Let me have her foot coverings! They are from Imez! I love their make!"

I take point. "Less lip, more speed, females! Move!"

We draw fire from the fleeing transports. The ship now takes aim at the two teams doing dizzying formations around it.

I demand, "Wep, where's my body cannon fledgling?"

My weapons-smith rockets to me. "In the game, Grandam!" In a fluid motion, she curls her small body into a tight ball, simultaneously charging her armor with her enhanced life energy. She hovers; her form radiates with light and power. I grab her gleaming body in my arms, securing her to me in my strong grip. I whip her form around to face our target.

The way is blocked by a rain of disruptor blasts from the craft.

"Hassa!" I curse. "I need cover for a clear shot."

My cluster tightens around me, we move as one force seeking a clear blast for Aylo, my body cannon.

For several palm-sweating minutes, Alpac Cluster draws fire from the Emera. A path between raining blasts opens for us.

The Grandam of the Alpac chimes in, "The way is yours, Grandam Emera."

I thank her. "Tava, Grandam Alpac."

I point the balled-up sister-flyer at the ship.

"Wep, paint the sky!" I order.

Aylo uncurls from her position, the front layers of her battle suit opens wide. A disruptive arc of energy rips from her small body, slitting the underside of the vessel as I fly guarded by my unit.

Its massive belly opens, gushing ichor.

Alga peels away. She rockets upwards.

"To the braincase! Come, Rish, Unu, Masi..."

Rish is too slow, for the last time. She is fried. Her body falls. No one laughs.

She disintegrates screaming in mid-air on the way down, armor and body turning to ash. I smell the burning of her feathers even through my helm. Sad. She had promise.

The Death Bringer fends off Alga and her team as they hunt for a kill shot to its braincase. It spews orange plasma while it searches for a clear blast with its tethered energy cannons. Its juices form glistening waterfalls down battle-ruined city towers.

Alga's team find their mark and hit it. Fire rages in one of its eyes, as its crew scrambles in confusion, buying us precious time.

Blue Squad's Command barks in our coms, "All squadrons, we are leaving! Fall back to the transports! Luck to you all. Make it home before the way is shut. We celebrate our dead tonight, don't become one of them!"

A massive teleportal opens in the southern sky.

More of their fighters enter. They are terrifying. Eight-limbed, Vis Stuvo crawler-craft surge towards us in rippling green waves.

Without warning, the city shields spark back to life. Vaporizing blasts from our attackers strike the invisible wall, transforming it into a canopy of gold light spanning the horizon.

They hold. It was what we'd all waited for.

The shields cancel out enemy communication from their queens. Their groupings break formation and stop firing, waiting for new orders, making them easy targets.

As the last civilian transports escape, the shields break. We use our flight packs at speeds high enough to rip some battle-worn feathers from our bodies.

We snatch up any ground forces left and jet inside the massive passage, allowing our enemies to follow.

Paths between worlds are used with caution. They are mysterious crossings as old as the multiverse and with their own perils. Powerful, strange creatures lurk there. Some are worse than the enemy we face, far worse. We enter the huge starlit chasm our Incantationists peel open for us. We have no choice.

Our transports and armed flyers zip through what is deemed the safest route home, through winding canyons formed by a lifeless planet a universe wide. It is older than anything known.

Luck is on our side, for a time.

Then, the glint of starshine disappears from around us. Gossamer tentacles drift down from the endless void above. We know this thing. We've had this horror happen to our people before. Every realm has scavengers, the Rungou Urso, is one.

Once the tentacles have scented those near death, our transports will be attacked, and ships cracked open. The wounded and dying are dragged to the orifice of some massive unseen host and feasted on. Their bodies will rain around us as we try to defend them. Shouts from every quarter are in my com: "Faster!"

Curses pour into my mind from hundreds of Commanders and Grandams.

I'm screaming, "Hassa acka, move your asses!"

Our pilots outmaneuver the appendages with breathtaking skills. In short time, we exit the portal into the pale blue skies of our home world. Tocca Base is there with three other massive battle temples. We are safe. No ships lost.

Our Incantationists use their powerful magic to shut the portal on the attacking hordes that follow, swallowing them whole forever.

My people cheer from the three worlds of the Oolran. We count this as a victory. We've crippled and humiliated our enemy. We lost a region to do it but saved so many. Great halls and battle temples on all our planets erupt in celebration to honor those that fought that day.

A short time later, Vis Stuvo Elites agree to our treaties, and leave us alone, as most attackers do.

I grin to myself. My kind are more trouble to deal with than it's worth.

My youngest was there, a fledgling student at Didasso, one of the great temples of knowledge in Graal. She'd refused early evac. It was her first fight. Her grey eyes could always find me in a crowd. I feel them on me, filled with love, studying my moves.

I wonder.

What does she think of me, her Umu?

{2}

When I open my eyes, there is Manhattan: the great Riverside church once more, and the lustrous sparkle of boats on the water. A hint of the Hudson's brine reaches me even at this distance.

A subtle fear burns my heart for what I could lose, but I will not let it destroy our time together.

Jeremiah meets me on his balcony. His body is tall and broad, his brown chest is bare. He wears tan satin sleep pants. They accent the walnut hue of his skin. The tight black curls of hair on his head and chin are touched with silver. A deep green cloth lays draped over his crippled left arm. The words, "Pop's Kitchen" is embroidered on it in gold lettering. He wipes his strong right hand with part of it as he studies me.

My man is kind, strong, funny and very handsome. Most of all, he sees me as one to be cared for, which only my sister-flyers have done. He already treats me with more focused affection than any male I've mated with. My male lot-mates, their minds are always clouded by their careers, schemes, and scandals. Like the rest of their brothers, they are so nonchalant about intimate relationships with females some feel the male sects could care less about us, and protect our worlds for their own ends.

Jeremiah smiles fondly. I smile back.

He caresses me with his eyes from the top of my violet feathered head, to my wings drawn up and back over my chair, to my bare breast and down to my feet. In that moment, it's not just the wind keeping my nipples hard.

"What is it?" I ask.

He shakes his head. Shirtless, his muscles look firm. A soft smile grows on his full lips, lighting his sleepy chocolate eyes.

Watching him admiring me is almost enough to make me forget about dinner, to yank his pants down and suck on his smooth muscle again, almost.

He laughs. "You are stunning. It's just too much having you naked all the time."

I flash a teasing smile. "I guess having huge blue wings are not a real distraction?"

He shakes his head.

His voice is smoky. "I'm fascinated by all of you woman, every inch, and ounce."

I look past him to the doorway of the kitchen, where the onion-meat smell taunts me without mercy. I shoot him a sidelong glance. "I must warn you. The food smells very good. If we wait much longer to eat you will hear from my stomach."

"That little thing?"

I smile, I rub my belly. "Ha, this little thing can snarl like the fiercest animal!"

He rolls his eyes, laughing. "Yeah, really? If you say so! God, I've got to cover you, or we will starve to death. Any move you make is keeping me fist hard."

He leaves again then returns with one of his robes. It is the color of wine, made of a soft suede-like plush.

"This one is my favorite. Your wings though..."

I lean forward and fold them down. They reduce in size before easing into the slim flesh pockets of my back. I stand. He slides the robe on me and kisses my neck when he's done.

I turn to face him.

"Man, how do they do that?"

I shrug, "We are born with them. As they grow, our defensive hormones and training combine. We trigger an instinctual defense response to reduce them, stripping them with our minds at their micro levels. Manipulating this section of our bodies is the first bit of magic we learn. They naturally enlarge to their full length once drawn them from their pockets."

He ties the sash around me. Then pulls out my chair. I take my seat.

"Our form of Magic, is the collective energy of my kind. Traces of it are scattered in every universe. We naturally tap it. I'm connected here by my training, by my biochemistry and my energetic body, my soul. My race shares a small amount of life force. Every part of me is attuned for seeking these trace elements scattered about since the dawn of our creation anywhere they are available."

He says, "It's amazing to me baby. There's nothing like you, not that I've ever heard of." He kisses me. The kiss is long and tender. He pulls away. He grins and points down, "See what you do to me? No, don't touch it! We need to eat."

The robe is large and comfortable. As I sit I rub my face in the lush fabric of it and breathe in his scent. Again, he leaves for the kitchen to return with our meal. He carries a platter of steaks, steamed greens and curried sweet potatoes in his good hand like a server at a dining hall. He lowers the tray to our table and takes his seat across from me.

He says, "Could we meet just after six? I want to take you shopping."

I ease a steak onto my plate with a prong. "I have my armor. It can look like any outfit."

He smiles thoughtfully.

"I adore you in it. It's that... There's a store near here with dresses I'd love to see on you."

I take up my glass again.

I say, "You'll only want to peel them off me." I sip the wine.

He nods, "Yes, oh yes."

He picks up his glass.

I laugh, "I thought you didn't like shopping."

He drinks, then says, "You mean with my ex-wife?" A dry laugh escapes him. "Essence Gleason needs a husband like she needs another Pomeranian puppy to carry in her damn Louis Vuitton purse. After she started making big money, she pretty much ignored me. I was there to hold her bags while she talked on the phone. We were married but stopped being..."

"Lovers?"

He nods, "Yep, you got it!"

He salutes me with his glass then takes a long sip.

He sits his drink down but keeps his fingers on the foot of the vessel.

A faraway look touches his face.

He says, "I should really explain our relationship to you baby. She and I met through a mutual friend. I adored her from the first time I laid eyes on her. She was fun, talented and beautiful, really beautiful.

"Back then, I had a tiny studio apartment further uptown. I worked armed security and did odd construction jobs on weekends. I was young, but I was always good with handling money just not enough for her to keep adding to her shoe and handbag collections, paying for cocktails for her and all her friends and buying take out all the time. She never cooked or cleaned, I did that. She kept any money she made at the lounge she sang at for herself. She had a few hits with her music. Her extended family was also made up of old singers from way back in the day and one-hit wonders, very bourgie. They never liked me, they told me I was too poor for her. I didn't listen. I loved her. I just couldn't give her the lifestyle she was used to in Atlanta. She loved me, at first.

Two years after we married, she went on a trip to LA with her manager, Carlos Mercina.

Mercina was good at his job and very well connected. He got her bookings, but I never liked the guy, and I should have listened to my gut. When she came back everything got way worse. She lost interest in us, nothing I did satisfied her anymore. She started drinking and having tantrums, breaking things, throwing her shoes like a spoiled brat, full of drama. It was tough to be around her. Even mutual friends stopped hanging out. I asked her what the hell was going on."

He laughs sadly, "She told me in LA, she could taste fame, she even dreamt about it. She said, 'I was in my luxurious home in Los Angeles. Everything was gleaming perfection, floor length mirrors on the walls, light was streaming in from huge windows. A fresh pot of coffee was delivered to me in bed. I laid naked in a pile of pillows, checked my emails and made my calls. Just as I was about to take my morning swim in the pool, I woke up. I looked around here and was like, Oh. This place. Again.'

She was my woman. I had to try to make her happy. I scored this condo for us by the skin of my teeth. I took out loans to help pay for better promotional material and more studio time. Nothing I did work. I felt alone. One day, I just stopped trying.

The war was still going on. Her family flipped out when I told them I wanted to go into the Army and serve my country, but not her. She just said, 'Well, that's good. You go do something important.'"

He shakes his head in a thoughtful way and takes another sip of wine. He sits his glass down and looks out over the water.

His voice is softer, "The army gave me purpose again. It worked, for a while. My second year in, we met up in Germany. It was clear. We cared for each other but, our thing wasn't working. On the last night, we made love. It was awkward. There was nothing from her but cold. After she left, I got a call from a good friend back at home. He told me she was sleeping with Carlos, her manager. I knew it was true but couldn't face it. We were deployed back to Iraq what could I do?

"About a month later, I got an angry call from her, she signed a contract for her first recording with a big company one day and found she was pregnant the next, I... I had to beg her to keep our baby. By the time Matthew was born, her career took off. She had more money than I could make in several years. When I got back to the states after my time in the Army ended, the apartment was empty of her things.

She and Mercina moved in together. I landed a job with the VA. It's good for me to find help for other veterans.

Funny thing though, she doesn't want to let me go. She told me just last week, 'The Music business is crazy. I'm glad you are such a good man. It's great to know there are still good ones in the world.' So, I guess things between her and Carlos are not so sweet."

He shrugs. "She sometimes uses our son to keep me in line. That really pisses me off. She's still explosive, drinks too much, and shows more interest in clothes than our son. I wanted a divorce and full custody for Matthew, but I couldn't fight her fame. She says a divorce means spending money and bad press. If I go for a one and make a stink in public, she told me she might leave the country with our son. Essence is a selfish bitch, but fame and money didn't make her that way. It was in her DNA all along."

He looks at me with a winsome smile. "Matthew hangs out here with me more and more. He's eleven now, a great kid, smart, brave, already a little soldier."

He grew quiet. He asks in a soft way, "Nat, I don't know how old you are, but you must be pretty up in age here on Earth. By the looks of you, I'd think you are really only 28 pushing maybe, 32 years old on your world. You got a man... a mate back home and maybe a few babies? You're too beautiful not to."

I smile and shake my head. "That is something I adore about you. You sense things, you are so perceptive. Yes. I've had many mates. I bore three female fledglings to term. Thoat, Lyvan, and Solr. The older two are already fighting in squadrons.

Solr, my youngest, is from my last union. She's showing solid ability as a Mystic. It's not common among female flyers. She wants to study magical defense.

Still, I feel she'll make a fantastic Incantationists.

Three of my young ones out of ten gestations lived. The rest of my little ones died inside me or vanished from my body."

He sits back, eyes wide. "Oh shit. You had ten..."

I look away. My voice softens.

"Yes. As I've said, Migdal's Scourge is still intense. Some young are never born. The magician that created it is long dead but still kills our children. Our time moves at a different pace than yours here. We are pregnant far longer. At times we wake to find our bellies flat well into pregnancy. The infant is just... gone, vanished. It is heartbreaking. Our cities still teem with us but many of my kind are centuries old compared to Earthlings. We constantly fight off attacks on our planetary system for our resources, but out of all the loss we encounter, a stillborn or vanished fledgling devastates us.

Anyhow, as for our male mates, they are chosen by lottery. There are two for every female Fighter, Combat Flyer, Incantationists, Wep-tech and the rest of the Twelve Orders of Protection.

Common folk do as they please, but even fewer of their young survive. They are not breeding as often as we do with only one mate."

He waves his hand in the air, "Wait, wait. You have two lovers picked from a lottery, right from your first..."

I nod, "Yes. It's all I've known. I've had two mates to live with every three cycles of Oolran Prime. I remember all of them but I'm fond of only a few. Our mates are more focused on moving ahead. Females are professional killers and tacticians, while our males have cunning mental abilities. They are skilled with science and what is deemed here as magic, our natural, energetic--occult forces. Sex is good but almost a chore for such great minds."

He looks at me, a moment longer with disbelief, then his eyes narrow. His jaw sets.

It is the first time I've seen a touch of anger in his expression. His eyes smolder.

"A lottery chooses who you have babies with? Nat, what kinda shit is that?" He looks away a moment like he is searching for the right words.

He turns back to me, his low voice simmers with his anger. "You fight for your people? You watch friends die, and raise your girls to be soldiers while your men stay safe and bored indoors and the sex they give you is like a chore to them? That sucks, Nat. It fucking sucks. I told you about how shallow Essence was. You are everything any sane man would want. You deserve better than that, damn it."

I am stunned. Slowly, I reach out, I caress his face. With his eyes closed, he turns his head, his lips find the heart center of my palm. He kisses my hand. I sense calm waft over him. He looks at his food with sad eyes. "I'm sorry to blow like that. You didn't create your system."

"It is fine, it is fine. Please, eat."

We eat in silence. His wounded limb has just enough life in it to pin the meat with a fork as he slices. His large, nimble right-hand offers me a morsel.

"You wish to feed me?"

"Yes, girl. That little belly needs lots of good food to keep it happy, right?"

Speechless, I lean in and take the tender chunk with my teeth. He smiles then gives me more slices of beef. In turn, I feed him some from my buttery sweet potato.

The quiet of the evening is strong. There are heavy feelings between us. When the music ends, I say, "Jeremiah. It is not all death that we face at my home. Our worlds are saturated with both natural and artistic beauty, we have much music and song. Our songs may not be as hopeful as your Stevie Wonder but they are just as lovely, just as... soulful."

He eases up from the table and walks into the living area. He changes the recording. The singer is female this time. Her voice is smoky, intimate.

She sings, "Whenever I'm alone with you, you make me feel like I am free again..."

Her words bring tears to my eyes. I'm surprised how deeply they touch me. I close them as I listen. I hear him return.

"Ki. Her voice reminds me of some of our singers."

When I open my eyes, he reaches for my hand, I slip mine into his. Moments later, we are in his living area dancing close, his weaker arm wrapped around me. His stronger hand is in mine, guiding my movements.

We move in an easy way. I lay my head on his shoulder inhaling his natural woodsy musk. He nuzzles the feathers of my head with his nose. His weak limb rests on my hip.

I've always loved dancing close. Females of my kind often do it with each other on the ground and in the air. We will dance with our mates if they are not too busy to attend gatherings. I'd never danced like this with a mate before, alone and with such easy intimacy.

We kiss; he kisses my throat. I step away from him and untie the robe. It slides to the floor, naked, I'm back in his arms, we dance again. My bare breast caresses his chest. My hips move in time with his, but the cloth of his sleep pants keeps his stiff member from contact with my skin.

"Nat..." He says my name softly. "Ten years?"

I nod. Tears burn my eyes. "Mm-hmm."

"Until you leave, I'm gonna love you good girl. You get back to me the next time you're on leave. Don't drift off to some other world to meet your Jedi Master or something, you hear me?"

"Is that an order, Sergeant?"

"Damn right it is, female. You're damn right."

My face tilts up to his, his mouth is on mine. He lands another to each of my eyelids, then my forehead. His good hand brushes my breasts. He glides it down to my belly it rests there.

A deep rumbling laugh escapes him.

"What?"

"The fierce animal in there, she full?"

I smile. "Yes, full and happy."

"Happy, really?"

"Oh, yes."

"What I got here ain't much woman. Shit, after some alien race puts you females through a meat grinder of a fight, you should be eating some big feast and getting drunk back at base with your sisters, having massages on vibrating pillows and carpets or something. Valkyries are talked about by the Norseman from a long time ago. If I remember, those big guys loved to eat and drink after a war."

It is my turn to laugh, "We have encountered many humans over time. We took men from around your globe. I am not so old to have taken them but I know of your Norsemen. Yes, we eat and drink fermented fire juices and have lots of pleasures with each other when not fighting. We do massage each other, often."

He laughs excited. A boyish gleam lights up his eyes. "Oh... oh, damn. You pleasure each other with sex and massage each other? All of you, fit and strong females, with wings and stuff?"

I look at him quizzically, "You relish the thought of females touching each other intimately? Our males are jealous of such activities. Is that a human delight?"

"For some, for me, well, yes! I think a man can learn a lot from watching females pleasure each other."

I tell him, "My sect of Blue Squad, the Emera Cluster, originate from Temple Base Tocca. It is where many of us celebrate our biggest victories. We are female so, of course, we know just how to make each other come. We are very skilled."

"You ain't lying there."

I laugh as my fingers brush his hard member poking at me. "Still... many of us yearn for a male mate that is as strong and passionate as we are."

A mischievous gleam enters his eyes.

He stops dancing. He takes my hand and leads me to another room.

Past his living area, in the center of the low-lit space, is his bedding. It is carved of wood, with a very large padding and has coverings in an attractive pile. It is large, dark and handsome, much like himself. He walks over to a big wax candle on a far table. He lights it with a striker from a top-drawer matching storage unit.

"Lay down there girl, I give a great massage. Can we have bath time in a few days?"

I climb onto the bedding. It is plush and deep. In some ways, it reminds me of my nests in my favorite nesting chambers back home.

"A bath together? I love the sound of it. Indeed, we shall. I think we may even get some washing done."

He walks over.

His voice is smoky, "Now, I'm not gonna make this sexual, this time."

I lay on my stomach, he is on top of me. I hear and feel him reach for something. There is a squirting sound, then his large comfortable hands are on me.

His one oiled hand glides over my ass and up my back as the crippled one stays on one firm butt cheek. He leans over his bare skin against mine and kisses the back of my neck. The air is scented with a fresh pleasant aroma I cannot name.

As if he can read my mind he tells me, "The massage oil is brown sugar and coconut."

Soft moans escape my lips. My eyes close as my form releases its tension to his firm but soothing grip. I rock my bare ass in a methodical way, pushing it up and down like a slow-moving wave on the ocean.

He laughs. "I said this won't be sexual! Damn it, Nat, you are not making this easy for me!"

He squeezes one of my ass cheeks with his weaker hand.

I purr, "My man, life can be difficult!"

I adore his laugh. His joy adds to wanting him inside me.

He shifts position suddenly, and sits on my butt, stopping its enticing movements. Now, we are both laughing. He reaches up again to my shoulders and back muscles. His weaker hand holds my waist but glides back in an unusual sweeping motion of its own.

His thumbs start a deep rolling pressure I find hypnotic.

My flesh melts for him.

"Mmm. That feels so delicious." My body and my mind are torn. "I want you but you are very good at this."

His voice is rich, "Rest baby. There's no rushing sex in my bed."

My breathing deepens as his hands discover a new, slow rhythm.

I drift off.

Startled, I wake. I sit up gasping at a strange dream that's already fled me. I look about. The candle is lit low on its platter. The air is still lush and warm with the scent of brown sugar and coconut.

I find no memory of the dream but it left a bad feeling inside me. Jeremiah is on his back next to me. His breathing is downy and slow.

I must shed my unease. I know just how I want to do so. My hand seeks my man's firm body.

I circle the nipples of his bare chest and place two fingers against his full lips. To my surprise, he kisses them.

"Are you asleep?"

His breathing changes. I am enchanted. In his sleep, he knows I'm there and responds. I wonder: does he dream of me touching him as I do it?

I drape my naked body over him. My hand glides to his cock. He stirs.

"You... take advantage of an unconscious man?"

"You must be ready for anything soldier. You've grown soft. I'll have to toughen you up. Starting with this."

"Naughty female."

He rolls over with a sudden burst of speed. A squeal of laughter erupts from me like a youngling as blankets go flying.

His cock is stiff in an instant.

"Gonna be on top this time. I don't think it's good to have you floating around here. My ceiling is not as tall, you'll hit it and that won't be sexy."

I aim my shaved sex at his stiff member, lifting my hips. He enters halfway.

"Hassa! Don't stop there man!"

He laughs as he thrusts. He stops again. I open my mouth to protest, and he starts in again.

I hiss and curse.

"You're cursing right? Damn, I love your foul language! I need to kiss that dirty mouth though."

We kiss as he hammers the dripping opening to my lock.

His cock erupts; he bites his bottom lip. Tears light the corners of his eyes as he withdraws, his pearl white fluid shooting from his staff.

I feel myself come in waves. The bed shakes. My body wants to rise up. I shut my eyes as I come. I cry out. His big hand covers my mouth; the other grips the headboard. My body shakes the bed, hard, then stops. Sweat drips from me.

"Are you... you alright?"

"I. Am. Perfect."

"Always happy to serve you, lady." He says then collapses to one side of me. I ease myself on top of his body like a drape.

Sleep takes us that way.

{3}

There is a strange burning smell that wakes me. I slide into his robe but don't tie it.

I sleep in the daytime, but not being in my own surroundings keeps me in a lighter state of rest.

I shuffle into his kitchen. Slumber clings to my every move, making my limbs feel like logs.

He laughs, "Good morning. You sleep hard baby."

"Fosteela." I answer him in the casual greeting of Temple Tocca.

"Yo! Is that good morning back at home? Here..."

He ties the robe. "I don't want you to catch cold. You don't die here on Earth from something so stupid."

I'm not used to smiling so early.

"Yes, fosteela is something like, "good morning" back at Tocca. Each base has a slight — " I yawn. "Variation of our mother tongue, Eochi."

Our hands glide around each other. My head lay on his shoulder. His good hand rubs my back. "Mmm... Then, I'll have to learn some Eochi from Temple Tocca."

I sniff the air. "What is that sour funk?"

"You calling my coffee sour?"

"Kihinju, yes. Sour funk."

"Try this." He passes me the steaming cup.

"Mmm... Tastes like sweet tree fungus and creamy dirt. Is it good for you?"

"It wakes you up."

"Why? Sleep. Is. Good. Mental training can wake you without smelling so nasty."

"Are you nocturnal? Like a bat?"

"On your Earth, yes."

"You get back to bed, Batgirl. I gotta work at the hospital. I work four days a week."

"I know. I've watched you."

"Will you meet me at six?"

"Shopping?"

"Yes, ah... kihinju," he says.

I smile and kiss his cheek.

"Ki." I purr.

He slides my hand to his crotch.

His voice deepens. "Tonight we have dinner at Cleopatra's Needle. A buddy of mine plays there... Then we go back to your place again?"

"Kihinju-ute, yes indeed."

He looks at me, eyes tight. "Come hell or high water, girl, I'm gonna be your man whenever you visit, for all the years of my life. On Earth, there will be no shitty lottery telling you who to sleep with. When you are here we live a normal life, okay?"

He lifts my hand and kisses my palm. He pulls me to him. I nuzzle his broad chest in our long embrace. I am blissful. There are no thoughts fluttering around in my head, just the desire to lure him back to bed.

"A normal life. That sounds like a promise, Sergeant."

His fingers trace the slim wing slits of my back.

"Well, sorta a normal life." He laughs. "Back to bed, you."

I awaken again at noon. I have several hours before I'm to meet with Jeremiah.

My body wants some small nourishment. Bleary-eyed, I find the kitchen and the cold-storage unit where, before dawn, Jeremiah had opened it for the cream he used in his dirt-nasty coffee.

I settle on the small eggs I find in a box and another of juice that reads it makes for a great breakfast. I butt-shove the door close and place my finds on the table. I open the egg box, take out a perfect little unit, tilt my head back and crack it open above my mouth. It is good, chilled and slightly creamy.

Next, I try to open the carton of juice, and though I follow how the design should work, I rip the top off the box. My strength has struck again, but this time, I'm able to enjoy my drink without it being plugged like the first wine bottle I opened. Still, I'm certain it is not the way to work the thing. In one hand I hold the top, and in the other is the container of golden juice. I shrug and take a sip. It is bright and delightful! I drop the ripped portion to the kitchen table, gather the box of eggs and the juice and carefully make my way inside. I sit them down on the small glass table near the long lounging chair to select some books from his collection. For the next few hours, I eat the eggs one after the next, drink the juice and breeze through several books. I do not understand much of it, but enough of what I read is enjoyable. His masculine aroma is deep in his garment. The warmth of his robe around me is so pleasant, I drift off to sleep for a short time after finishing the last egg.

When I rise, I put the half-full, torn juice container back in the cold unit and leave the empty egg box full of shells on the table. It is just enough until our night meal. I've read Jung on his provocative mysteries of the mind and think how close he was; one book warning of the use of adorable drone craft in battle; a wonderful brief history of the thoughts of a Roman Emperor — Marcus Aurelius, one I've heard of back at home — and finished a cookbook on crafting stews and quick meals.

I make a mental note to try one for my new mate at my dwelling. I notice there are a few small drone craft on his shelves.

I grin as I hold one of the handsome, dish-sized mechanicals. Gingerly, I place it back, striking its funny little propeller. It spins at my touch.

I think, *Sergeant and Pilot.*

I soon discover the waste and bath-shower units and spend a refreshing few hours in the little rain. He does not seem to use as many fragrant soaps and washes as we do. There is only one style of each. I use all that he has. I plan to replace them with a basket of items from my reserves. With the spell I shall teach him, the basket will replenish itself, drawing from our residual magic and hidden store the way such simple things should. My kind spends days in cleansing pools and at bathing falls when not in battle. No one, male or female, should be without good-smelling, foaming cleansers.

{4}

I return to my keep as the sun sets. Dressed in my armor, I enter my sanctuary. I fly in from a side window and take the stairs to the main floor. It is the first time I've entered the Cathedral in decades.

The church has transformed into an elegant place of worship. It reminds me of a smaller version of our flying battle temples or fortress retreats, but more ornate. There are images of angels all about. I miss our worship of the elements, our buildings fly not only as sentries but to connect with the massive energy centers on each of our planets. Drawing strength from each other and our worlds, is grounding to me. There is security and comfort knowing when we die, we are one with our magic in every realm. It is not only what our Seekers and Frey Priestesses teach us. It is what we know.

We meditate, chant and cultivate our connection to the higher power within us, it rapidly heals us, and gives us long life. We talk to our dead and to our ancestors often and often, they talk back to us. Though our technological levels dwarf that of humans on Earth, we listen when our trees or ancient stone speak, some of us far more than others. The Oolran are linked to all of this by our body chemistry and spells, meditation, and powerful vows. We are a rough but often a brilliant and beautiful people.

Studying one of the larger stone angels, sword in hand wings out stretched, my heart aches for home.

I hear someone approach. A man in flowing white vestments greets me.

His voice is kind. "Can I help you?"

"Thank you, yes. If I were to make a donation of clothing to the poor, where would I drop off the package?"

"You walk to the front of the building and head down three flights to the offices. There is a donation bin in room A10."

Down the stone stairs, there are a few visitors, people praying as the organist practices. I find the corridor, then the room.

I want to dress in something simple for our first time shopping together. Visitors in civilian wear and acolytes in simple robes drift by me, ignoring me in my armor as I make my way down the elegant hall to the stairs.

In the donations area, I tell the helpers that greet me, "I have a friend that needs a few items of clothing for her stay in the city. She is shy about asking for help. Can I pick out a few things for her? I'll leave a donation."

He says, "Sure, no worries."

I choose dark leggings, a large long sleeve shirt, simple black footwear and a cream wrap for my head. Once I remove my armor, the spell will be broken. Anyone could see me for what I am. I leave a century note in the donations box.

As I walk on, gentle pangs of home continue to tug at my heart. The soft smells of incense wafting after me makes me long for Tocca Base. My cluster, the Emera, would sometimes float together cleansed and naked, reaching a dreamy, meditative state breathing in specialized intoxicants. We'd hover with others like us, fresh from battle after battle, in one of countless Calming Chambers. Grandams and commanders later meet, drawing factious battle strategies after water rituals on the sub-levels.

I so enjoy all of it.

Yet, I think of my new mate's hand in mine, dancing, his sent, his laughter when he holds me close. How natural and comforting his presence is to me.

As I spot my secret entrance I hear him say, "Come hell or high water, girl, I'm gonna be your man whenever you visit, for all the years of my life. On Earth, there will be no shitty lottery telling you who to sleep with. When you are here we live a normal life, okay?"

We are a perfect match, his mind and heart is strong and brave, he is open to the magic of my soul.

A mate of my own.

I will not allow this longing for home to last. I want to be here, now enjoying every moment I am able with him.

{5}

At my keep, I dress fast, occasionally glancing at my favorite armor on its stand. I keep four complete suits as we are taught. The suits are silvery blue in color, the black glyph of Emera Cluster boldly emblazoned on their chest on the back and at the tops of the jointed hip. Hundreds of glowing crimson sigils are carved into the metallic shell and into their matching, aerodynamic helms. It helps that my Wep-tech Aylo is brilliant at her craft.

I rescued Aylo from a scandal that would have ended her career like that of Mundi, my second in command before Alga. Mundi and Aylo became lovers. There were harsh consequences, Mundi was stripped of everything but is now content working as an Investigator. They would have lost much more. I never regretted the decision to help them.

Almost never. Aylo is sometimes a pesky creature.

I am trained that if the suits are damaged off-world, I can cannibalize what cannot be repaired, though no Alien aggression has been reported on Earth. There are no threats to the small blue planet, but the ancient records here are lost. No one is very sure on the subject.

The clothing from the church is soft but common, machine-made. Our normal modes of dress are grown, woven or spell made; they are silky and metallic, or sheer, but almost as strong as armor. Fully dressed, I wrap the scarf about my head.

My limbs look long and shapely in the leggings. I caress them a moment, lifting one leg in the air and easing my palms down it, then down the other. The large, golden shirt falls off my shoulder to one side.

I check the mirror before I leave. I like the way my nipples poke its buttery material.

I push up the sleeves. Grinning, I think of him kissing me there. I feel more naked dressed this way. I fear he may judge my choices too peculiar. I laugh. This is packaging for him. No matter what I wear, the real prize for him is underneath these garments.

I ease my feet into the dark, simple foot coverings and make my way to the window. The opening in the back of my shirt allows my wings out. I drop, then coast to the ground below, unseen.

On the crowded walkways, I maneuver past people, not looking at them. My life's energy is high. I feel young and glowing inside.

Soon, I wait outside the medical facility for him. It's only a few moments until he exits and spots me. Other males walk with him. They pat him on the back and become full of smiles as they talk and look at me. He moves away from them, striding toward me.

He wears dark, snug denim pants; a silvery white, long-sleeve cotton shirt; dark leather foot coverings and a black leather jacket tossed over the shoulder of his working arm.

The other he keeps in a dignified ease bent in front of himself.

Reaching me, he slides his jacket over his bent arm, the other glides around my waist. "Look at you, that's how you do it, baby."

"Do what?"

"Look easy and beautiful. Your eyes alone can melt a man's heart." He leans to me for a kiss. Our lips connect for a long moment. Our open displays of affection reach me inside and flood me with warmth. I am happy to be with him; it feels normal.

At the dress shop, we are treated by an attractive, dark-skinned woman with flame-colored dreadlocked hair.

"Can I help you?"

She leads us into a changing area. I choose items by color, he looks at their style and cut.

Through a crack in the door, she passes me gold-colored sandals that bind my feet in a comfortable and strange way. Each time she hands me a dress, he peeks in at me a few moments later.

I manage to keep my wrap over my head whenever the saleswoman appears with a new garment. He peeks in again.

I stand naked except for the golden heels.

"Shit. You're so beautiful." He steps in and slides both his hands down my body. He kisses my sexflower. I detect the woman coming and shove him hard out the door. He nearly falls out.

He is laughing as he speaks with her about another outfit.

She seems not to notice I'd shoved him away.

"Do you have that one in white?"

When she leaves, he peeks back inside. I am dressed in the silver frock.

He comments as his eyes quickly size me up: "Wow!'

He reaches out to touch me as I'm admiring myself in the finer mode of dress and material. I swat him away and close the door.

I choose three slim dresses, one crimson, another in violet, one in silver and matching foot coverings.

It is hard to decide which one.

I take all three, the silver strappy foot covers, a set of sandals in gold and a pale wrap sprinkling with tiny crystals that catch the light. He puts a card of commerce on the table.

"We can drop the bags off with my doorman before dinner."

I choose to wear the silver one and the new crystal head cover out of the store for that evening. The dress is long-sleeved hugging my nipples. It fits me like a second skin to my mid-thighs. My body looks made of liquid metal.

I laugh to myself.

Yes, I feel more naked dressed this way.

{6}

The restaurant is large, warm and inviting with dark wine-colored walls and small tables. Well, dressed adults are lit by little jewel-toned table lamps. They laugh and enjoy their conversations. The music is strange but pleasant, lively, with just four players. Their sound makes the place even more inviting.

My mate tells the greeter, "I'm on the guest list for two, under Jose Martinez."

"Ah, this way please."

"What do you think Nat?"

"Mmm, it smells very good."

My stomach grumbles in an obscene way.

He and our guide stop to look at me in surprise.

I shrug. "I warned you."

My mate laughs and takes my hand.

We sit near the performance area.

He tells me, "Damn, I needed this. Every day, I wrestle with the government to help our vets. The ones like me with injuries, or with PTSD, or other mental health issues. It's never ending. My manager can't hire an assistant for me."

A server comes and pours a bubbling fluid into our glass. "This is from Mr. Martinez."

He takes a long sip from the glass. "Thank him for me. Slap his forehead too. He will understand."

He turns to me. "I understand that we can't hire right now, not at the pay rate for a professional, but he won't think twice about asking a local college intern for way less. Our vets are a handful. Lots of guys and girls trust me but they need so much. I love my work but fuck! I'm not a magician! Today, I so wanted to say 'get me an intern damn it!' I'm not a fucking machine."

I shake my head.

"I so adore your flexible language. A fucking machine sounds pretty good! Anyhow, lover, I'm glad you take care of your soldiers. Even Golgorn outcasts are healed on my world if there is enough left to heal."

He looks distant. "We have a good system in this country, but it's not enough. We could do far better. There are many places in the world that are far worse than this country at taking care of wounded warriors. Still, too many of us have to hack through the bureaucratic bullshit for the most basic things."

He looks at me a moment and blinks as if shaking off a dream. He brightens. "God, you look amazing, bae bae. Even with clothes on it's so difficult not to touch you. I love pushing it, though. Wanting you is like fire inside me on a cold day. It's a great feeling. I haven't felt such a good burn in ages.

Forgive me for going on about my work. You only have two weeks here, there are more important things."

I give him a sly look. "You have far more restraint than I. I could attach my body to yours for the next several days and only then be deeply satisfied."

His eyes grow wide in surprise. He sits back, tosses his whole drink down.

He laughs. "I may have to test that! I mean, at least go a whole day just naked, pounding and grinding, covered in sweat."

I place my fingers to his lips in a teasing way, he kisses them. Then I take up my glass.

"What we are doing is to me richer than physical intimacy alone. I am adoring this courting... um, wooing? Which is the right word?"

He grins his teeth are white and dazzling. "Wooing, I think that is Renaissance or Victorian or some such! Well, I'm wooing you baby, and I plan to do it from the top of your pretty feathered head to your toes. I'm gonna treat you the way a man — a mate should... Shit, Nat. There is so much I want to share with you. "

I drink and try to hide my pleasure at his words. I'm melting inside. I don't know how much of it he can see in my eyes.

He shakes his head. He says, "I won't try to stop you, but you leaving will be the most painful moment I've had in ages and ages." He pinches between his eyes a touch of emotion flits in his eyes before he turns away. He looks away at the musicians.

The music is very playful and rich. My man points with his thumb. "That's him, the dog." His friend on the conga drums nods in our direction. An older man, with golden skin, muscular arms, dark t-shirt, white pants and shoes. A winning smile beams our way from underneath a milky white hat.

Jeremiah raises his glass in acknowledgment. "Look at that grin, like the devil! Martinez is already sizing you up. He's gonna try to sweep you off your feet the moment I turn my head to sneeze."

I look at him surprised.

"He is a friend. Why would he..."

He takes a drink before answering.

"He loves beautiful women. He feeds off passion, he's always hungry."

The server stops by to take our order.

When she is gone, he leans in.

"Nat... I got to ask you. Why has Earth not been attacked?"

"It may have been attacked."

"What? When?"

I tell him. "Records and evidence were lost after catastrophic incidents in your history. Floods and mass extinctions swept away libraries and historic collections. If we found you, we are certain others have. But lost interest for whatever reason. Your planet is pretty well hidden. Even asteroids don't strike here often. There are beings that need specific resources that may not be found here. It is also difficult to travel between realms for many. We made it our focus to travel that way using its dangers to our advantage, but it is still not easy. There are some murderous creatures on those paths. Often, intelligences from distant universes don't communicate with each other. Not that they can't; it just ensures their safety to stay in seclusion."

He nods. "I'm sort of a documentary junkie. I used to read a lot when I was younger. Now I'm more drawn to visuals, watching and reading on my computer. You are right about things getting wiped out every few thousand years. Every culture has recorded a great flood or massive die off. Mm-hmm. Once, it happened in a huge way. The Toba Eruption. A super-volcano caused a volcanic winter. Only around four thousand humans survived. Now, look at us. We are like a swarm."

I nod. "Your kind may need to go off-world or, live out on your seas. It's strange to me you've not yet done either already. Your people travel the oceans even now.

We build sky cities in the In-Between, land and sky. The cities on the ground are farming and fishing and manufacturing."

He leans into the table, eyes wide. "Floating cities, I fantasize about that. How?"

"Our mystic-architects have their secrets."

There is a break in the music. People are applauding.

The slim group leader on a brass horn calls out. "We'll be back after the break, y'all. Enjoy the house special, peach cocktails."

Martinez steps away from his drum.

He approaches the table. His hand lifts mine to his lips.

In a move that makes me turn my head in sudden laughter, my man's hand slides between the gap of my hand and his friend's lips.

"Ay dios mio, primo! Why the hell you gotta snuff my fire? My lips almost touched your big ass hand!"

My mate tells him, "Hey, I kiss her hand, not you. She doesn't need your cooties."

The golden skinned drummer ignores him. He asks, "What is your name, elegant mama?"

I say, "Nat. Nat Emera." It is my turn to improvise. I steal a glance at Jeremiah's face. He looks impressed.

I add, "I have enjoyed your drumming."

His smile is charming. "A woman of taste! Nat. A hard name for a beauty with sultry eyes and delicate hands. A word of advice, watch out for his ex! She's vicious, she likes throwing things, like her shoes, silverware, dishes. I had to break up something with her and her man Mercina here last week. They got into something over a girl he's talking to. Did you hear Jerry?"

Jeremiah almost snarls. "Oh hell no. I don't keep up with her that way, but thanks. Last I heard, she was in anger management classes. I don't want her like that around my son."

Martinez nods, "I thought you should know. She needs to lay off those peach cocktails. Anyhow, it's good to see you with a beautiful and level-headed mama." He blows me a kiss from his palm.

"Hope to see you again, Nat Emera."

{7}

Once outside, we walk hand in hand a while.

We turn west along the quiet of the park near the Hudson River. We pass under a bit of crude construction for a row of buildings. He takes my hand and folds it over his weak arm. It pulls me closer. "You walk together like this when a meal and the company has been... how do you say it? It's been pleasurable."

I should be smiling, but a smell hits me. My body freezes. It is disturbing, I can't place it. No, it is not that I can't place it. It is that the scent is on the wrong world. It is the smell of a race of creatures I'd fought once before. It is a strange, damp, burning aroma not of this realm.

A searing voice cleaves the air between us. "Flyer..."

I freeze. Jeremiah stops with me. He looks at me in a curious way but says nothing.

Then, we both see it. It is a heavy shambling thing. It rises up slow from the shadows, studying us.

Its voice is hissing, hypnotic.

"Funny to see one of your kind here. It will be a pleasure to end you."

The large humanoid form bursts out of the darkened alley. Four glowing red orbs rise up from stalks on its back. Its dark purple head is bald like an old man, but eyeless. It shows us a horrible grin wrapping around most of its head, full of bladed teeth. It reaches to its chest as it moves.

I squeeze my mate's hand.

"Run."

We take off. I glance back, knowing what it is, but needing to see it. It is an Ickululuru scout. It being here offends every part of me. Shirtless, it pulls at the seam in its rib cage, it gives with loud cracks.

My wings spring out and I launch up, away from my date. Acid gushes from its chest cavity, directed at me. The air burns with searing metallic fumes from its gastric juices. My flight is a blur at battle speeds. It follows, locked onto my movements. I glance back, hoping to spot my mate. A sickly green light shows from inside its chest cavity as a stream of acid projects from it.

Behind it, I glance Jeremiah moving stealthily.

I'm maneuvering to the water's edge. My dress is torn and about my waist, my breasts are out, but I ignore my near nakedness. I don't dare flee. They live near water and devour prey alive as the acid burns them. Now that we've uncovered its lair, it will kill all the civilians it can before it feels safe enough to rest again. I've seen them at it.

It's got to die.

It takes a breath, preparing for another blast at me.

I see Jeremiah snatch something from the construction site. He runs, jumps forward, and stabs the thing in its back with an iron rod. The rod emerges from its chest but misses its hearts. He grips the rod and wraps his strong legs around the creature's waist. Its big arms are flailing, trying to reach behind itself.

It is unable to inhale again. I drop down on it and entwine my legs around its sightless head and neck, then I wrap my arms around its head, gripping it with all my strength.

"Jeremiah, saulif ock! Let go, now!"

He jumps away and I flap my wings, hard. I flip over the rails yanking it and my body over.

"Nat! God! God, no!"

Its weight carries us down towards the dark water below.

{8}

My winged body hurtles towards the churning water of the Hudson River. Less than an hour ago my lover, Jeremiah and I, were having an enchanting candlelit dinner. Now, I descend into the black waters off Riverside Drive.

I grapple with the acid spitter as I fall. It emerged from a dark alley, proud to expose itself to me and my human lover. The beast would kill hundreds before it felt safe enough to slip back into hiding. It must be stopped. I will usher the foul thing to the void of Death myself.

"Nat! No!" Jeremiah screams over and over from the railing of the night covered park. Helpless, he watches my fate. I wish I could comfort him, but there is no time.

I know what water does to my assailant's exposed insides.

Got to keep its chest cavity open long enough for it to drown.

The waves will be brutal. My body is tough, battle-ready at all times. I heal rapidly, but there are limits. My lungs and organs are still vulnerable. I know I'll have one chance at this, or succumb to the tides and drown.

"You don't die here on Earth from something so stupid." My lover said just that morning about me catching a cold. He'd wrapped his robe close around me to keep me warm.

No, my sweet man, I won't die here, in front of you from something as stupid as drowning. I swear it.

We slam against the rushing waves. The beast lands first. Its body takes the impact as I'd planned. Its bones crack but more is needed to kill it. In an instant, darkness swallows us whole.

Swirling cold currents force us downstream.

The glow of its opening is the only light in the surging waters. It tries to yank the bar out of its chest. I hold it in place as water hammers our bodies. The bar is knocked free and I grip its chest cavity open with my hands, my legs intertwined with its limbs. I lose my breath just as the glow in its hearts die.

I can hardly see but I instinctively know which way is up. I let its carcass go and shoot skywards with all the energy I have left.

Channeling the power in my damaged wings and the core of magic in my body, I rocket forth, breaking the surface. My form rises above the tree line, then tumbles out of the sky to land on the soft earth of New York's Riverside Park.

My body is wrecked, limbs and ribs broken, but I've taken worse. My breathing is almost nonexistent.

Though, already, I sense I am healing.

It feels like hours when I hear my name.

"Nat! Be alive, just be alive!"

I take deeper, painful breaths as he pulls me into his arms. I don't know how bad my face looks but I'm folded in a tangle of broken limbs. My eyes are screwed shut from the pain. He feels me shifting; he sees my parts re-form into place at an astonishing rate. He lays my body back on the soft dirt.

"Jesus, Jesus..."

My healing factor is in overdrive, damaged limbs pull back into place with cracks and re-breaking.

I wish I could pass out from the pain but I do not. Small sobs, moans and hissing escape my lips. My eyes flutter open. His handsome dark features look older with worry, his clothes are covered in dirt and torn in spots from struggling with the creature.

He's holding my hand now that my fingers are straight. I am naked except for my silver foot wraps. My wonderful new dress washed away. As usual for my kind, there is hardly any bleeding.

He leans over my face and kisses my lips.

He says, "Rest... rest."

Releasing my hand, he leaves then returns with a large, coarse drape he's found to wrap me in. He gets me up. I lean on him, grunting, letting out short cries of pain as he coaxes me to move. We make it to a street just outside the park.

Jeremiah hails a cab. He gives his address to the driver. "Drive fast, man."

"Is she alright?"

"She's... having a bad night."

My wings want to retreat into my body to heal faster, but they are wrapped around me, pinned under the drape.

I'm moaning.

My mate's deep voice is steady. "I got you, baby. Almost home."

I pass out.

When I wake, I feel him gently petting my head. It's in his lap as we lay on his floor, blankets covering us. Candles are lit as well as soft, comforting incense. Coconut, I think. I feel better.

He looks serious.

"You could have told me how fast you heal."

My voice is tired, weaker than I'm used to.

"I never thought we'd face danger here. I'm sorry to scare you. So sorry."

My stomach makes a small grumbling sound. Healing from life threatening injuries always makes me hungry.

"I hear your stomach. She needs to eat, yeah?

"Yeah..."

He plants a lingering kiss to my forehead. "That's my girl. You're alive, baby, that's what matters."

I look at his face. Smiling, tears roll down his dark cheeks. I am surprised at the mix of emotions I feel. I am grateful that we are both alive and together.

My own tears come. "I... adored my dress. It was the first gift you gave to me. I am sorry to ruin it."

He says, "I loved you in that dress but know what? I love you alive."

His words nurture me. I feel my heart swell. I smile a little. He kisses my forehead again then my lips.

"That was some nasty shit you fought, baby."

I give him a stern look. "I refuse to die in front of you. I'll not have our last memory together be so horrible. Still, if it had burnt you, or hurt you in any way, I'd made it suffer more."

I reach up to caress his serious features with the tips of my fingers.

"Ickululuru scouts — acid spitters — hide. Shooters like that one knock us from the sky. That rod you forced into it kept it busy. It gave me leverage."

He kisses my fingertips and whispers, "Hush. I'm taking the next few days off from work. You get better, you just do that, hear me? That's an order, Grandam."

"Kihinju sergeant." I whisper.

He eases me into his bed and for three days, he feeds and periodically, massages me. Again, I've always healed with the help of other female flyers from Emera Cluster. My bedmates like the two I have now, Edel and Alazar, would often visit me in the Healing Sector, they'd say kind words or hold my hand or bring gifts of comfort, balms and lots of fermented drink, but that's all. The level of care Jeremiah shows me is as attentive as any trained Metaphysician's Acolyte in my realm. He's bandaged the femur of my left leg, broken in two. It needed much more attention.

I walk on unsteady limbs to the wash room to empty my bowels. Jeremiah is suddenly there at the doorway each time to help me back to our rest. I wake in his bed chamber in late afternoon. He wears a pale blue shirt and dark sweatpants. There is a soft smile on his face and a delicious smelling bowl of stew in his hands. He sits near me and takes up the stew from the bowl with a scoop.

"Open wide, bat girl."

I laugh and eat some stew. "Do you like the bats of this world?"

"Yes. Anything that kills pests and bugs I like. You have bats on your worlds?"

He readies more stew for me to eat.

"Yes. They are intelligent and grow very old. Most are as big as we are. They're great hunters and very wise."

His voice is warm. "You get well and grow old. You'll be a wise old bat someday. Here you go."

He feeds me again.

His features grow sadder than I'd seen. Not as sad as in the park but close enough. His voice is tinged with grief.

"I wish I could be there with you, to fight beside you, protect you. Just don't forget me. Okay?"

"Never." I tell him.

I eat a little and sleep a lot, I wake that night, his arm is around me, he's is giving off a light snore. I feel much better, more myself. I rub the strong dark arm around me.

I say in a soft voice, "Hadi dia groutu."

"Mmm?"

"Never I'll forget."

He kisses my forehead and drops back to sleep. The blankets are warm like my nest. I let slumber take me again.

The next morn, I smell the stink of coffee. My leg support is off, my limb looks fully healed.

He enters the room, mug in hand.

"Hey baby girl. Fosteela."

I smile. "Fosteela." I sit up slowly. "What segment of day is it?"

"It's early, 10am. Want eggs?"

"Ute. Indeed."

I add, "Today, I want to walk in the park again. I will move slower now but I think I shall like the pace. It seems life here is more enjoyable that way."

Later, he carries a wooden basket with food and drink he'd packed. He is dressed casually in a black cotton shirt, denim pants and jacket and simple foot coverings. I wear one of his shirts, a matching pair of old jeans and my silver sandals. Everything is large and slouchy on me but he seems to adore it, rolling the sleeves of the shirt and the bottoms of my pants.

After a short ride down on the buildings lift, he introduces me to his door guard. A stout, pale-skinned, well-muscled man in a dark suit greets us at the entrance.

"Mike, this is Nat. She's staying at my place for a few days. Anything she orders out for, please drop it off at my place for her."

"Sure thing, Mr. Gleason."

"Do you need me to grab a cab for you guys?"

"Naw. I got this. Thanks."

"Have a great time."

Once outside with him, my legs are shaky. He keeps his arm about me as he hails a car. "Central Park, 59th Columbus Circle."

We exit the car and enter the park. Eventually we take a dirt path past some amusements for children, a brightly painted carousel of wooden animals, and vendors selling bubble guns for little ones.

He leads me through the open gate of a small fence to a striking green grass and clover field. People are playing all manner of games, sparring with each other with wooden and toy weapons, chasing and throwing balls and discs.

"This is the Sheep Meadow. I love this area. I come here to chill."

I look at him, surprised. "To freeze?"

His laugh is sudden, loud and charming. He looks at me shaking his head. "To chill means to hang out and unwind. I lay out on a blanket rest my head under the open sky. I watch people enjoying themselves, I sometimes daydream."

"Day. Dream. About what?"

"All sorts of things. How to make my drones do cool stuff, about the kind of life I'd want to have when I'm older if I hit the lottery, about floating cities. When you leave, I'll daydream about loving beautiful naked black girls with wings. I never hung out here with a lover, baby. You'll be my first."

"I am honored. Dreaming is sacred where I am from."

We make our way through others stretched out on blankets in leisurely fashion, eating, listening to their devices on tiny ear pieces, reading from books, sleeping or kissing. He sits the basket down under one of many big shade trees. I lean against it as he spreads out a large bright colored cloth from the basket. He sits, he gestures for me to be with him.

I look about.

"Did everyone eat the sheep? Is this the celebration after?"

He falls back on the blanket, laughing. "That's just the name! This happens here almost every day. It's Saturday, part of the weekend. It's a time when people can really enjoy being together. Come here you."

I drape myself over his body. I fit well.

His tone is serious and quiet. He says, "I already know the beat of your heart, baby. You're still not well. You can't go home like this, can you?"

I glean the concern in his soft black eyes. "I must go home." I sit up and look him in his eyes. "I am sorry to leave this city, to leave you."

I study the place. There are couples practicing fighting arts, playing and performing graceful meditation dances that feel familiar to me. Even with our advancements we embrace our natural forces. In my realm, many of the trees and stones are so old they give off a resonance as we live among them, shaping them and other materials for our dwelling. They sing or whisper wisdom to us. Here, the trees are very young. No one is sitting with head bowed, listening to them, but they may have not much to say.

Still it is a wondrous site for my eyes. All around the field males and females wrestle, chase their children and each other laughing in the short grasses. Many of the males look like they are enjoying those moments as much as their females and young. The modest green space is ringed with towering old buildings under a perfect blue sky.

Tears sting my eyes, watching.

He sees my tears.

I rest my head against his chest and turn my face away.

"Hey."

I turn back, he kisses me and brushes my tears away with his good hand.

"I think I love you baby girl, like a lot. You can always rest when you come back to Earth. We don't need to do nothing but make love and dream. Okay?"

I am trembling. I'll lose this fragile way of being in only a few days' time.

I say, "I want this. I didn't know I wanted such things so strongly with a mate, until I met you."

He laughs. "Tell me about it."

We stay in the park until dusk, laughing, talking, napping and kissing. We eat a small meal of sandwiches and drink what he calls sangria. It is like wine but cold and full of cut fruit.

"You made this when I was resting?"

"Yeah. I love cooking up good eats."

"I shall cook for you soon."

"At your place?"

"Yes."

"If I eat it, will I grow wings out my back?"

"I cook well," I laugh, "but not as good as that."

{9}

The next evening, I feel strong enough to leave for my keep. I fly but I am still too weak to carry him from his balcony. Inside, I unblock the nondescript stone doorway and cast the spell revealing a passage in the outer wall on the side of the building to the stairs, an alternate escape route leading from my lair.

When he arrives, I am flat on my back in a pile of cushions and colorful rugs, exhausted. He sits on the pile beside me. He leans over and kisses my forehead. He sits back and pulls out his small communications device from his jeans.

"Rest. I got dinner."

"What are you doing?"

"I'm ordering Chinese. I have a special relationship with the place and the delivery guy."

"Delivery, here?"

He ignores my question and asks, "Spicy sautéed eggplant and steamed shrimp dumplings for you?"

"Shrimp and something spicy and saucy, yes! A delivery, how?"

He says, "You need surprises baby, good ones that don't jump out of the darkness and try to eat you. Trust me, no one will know about this place. I got this."

He places the order and slips his device into a slim pocket of his jacket. He rises. I watch as he looks about. With care, he places a shaggy lamb's wool skin over me, taking it from it's place on the far wall. I like seeing him here, in his jeans, dark leather jacket, and short tan work boots. He looks back at me, his eyes shimmering in wonder. There wasn't enough time to study my space the first night we'd had pleasures. He'd awoke in my nest and dressed quickly. I flew him home to be in time for his work at the veteran's care facility. He turns a slow pirouette, looking every which way. His eyes have the dreamy quality of wonder in them. I study him, taking measure of his countenance. He is strong and both rustic and modern. He fits my refuge, and my life well.

I smile warmly. He's strong, rustic and modern, he fits here.

"This retreat is a small version of my dwelling back at Tocca Base."

His focus rises to the soft glow three levels above. "Wow, the ceiling is way up there. I see a platform and more of those light globes. Is that like a lounge?"

I sit up, taking my time.

"Yes. Up there are some of my favorite scrolls, clay tablets and other forms of communication from my travels. I never douse the illumination fully, I keep it lit low. The orbs there can't be seen from the windows. When I arrive, it gives me a welcoming feeling."

He laughs. His voice is soft. "Many people do the same, we leave a light on when not at home. Yeah, it helps keep thieves away but maybe we all want to feel welcomed, like someone waited up half the night for us."

I beam to myself. How good it is seeing these things anew through his eyes. This, I did not expect.

"I still sometimes light a few piles of candles."

"Mmm. I feel you, I would too. I like it very much. It's magical yeah but it's also... peaceful."

Without looking, he reaches out as he passes me and brushes my bare arm with his fingertips, and we both know what is passing between us, that nothing more needs to be said. *Perhaps*, I muse, *but I'm not at all certain we understand this, either. Maybe, we don't need to.*

He walks over to the multiple suits of armor hovering just a few inches above the floor. His fingers trace the spells Aylo placed into them igniting their protections for a brief moment. Sensing no threat, they dim.

Over time, my carvings of protection spells have worn into the stones. I'd casted sharing my life force with them. They shift and twist on the walls in muted colors that would become dazzling if I'd allowed them. They are of higher skill the more they are hidden. I'm not an exceptional spell-caster, I like seeing my work move about. He turns spotting the one feature in that space, a freestanding wall in the next smaller room. A towering wall of silver.

"Is it all real silver?"

"Some Earth metals conduct our magic better than others some are easier to shape but can be stubborn. Gold is that way, silver or iron are best. It is my food stores and other needs."

Carved with massive rugged glyphs it has smaller draws by the hundreds with little crystal windows above a slim bar on each to pull them open. "My storage. Each draw hold items I need to sustain myself, each connect to small dimension only used for storage near each world we visit."

He shakes his head. "Damn, bet that's worth a small planet right there."

His attention turns to one of the smaller three hovering tables made of a hardwood that grows in mid-air. Two orbs follow him as he pulls the near weightless ebony colored thing over near to where I lay. He places two wax candles in their silver holders there. He pushes it down to the floor where we can eat off it, then sits with me.

"How do you light them?"

"My life force. My magic. With a spell, I release a small part of my being."

I whisper "Illoutu." The word for firelight. I blow from the tip of my finger and point at the candles in a deliberate way. Tiny flames rise from them.

He laughs. His dark face is lit beautifully. A comforting feeling rises from within me and floods my being.

Love. Yes. Oh, yes, that's what this is. I smile.

Not long after, I hear a high-pitched whine. The small craft hovers outside my window, clutching a package.

"A drone. Yours?"

He guides the thing in with its package. It lands in my nest. He walks over the edge to collect it.

"Mine. They are used to it at the take-out spots I order from. I showed them videos about drone delivery and they all dig it. I use my cell phone and the app to navigate it. They are used to it now at Sun Dragon. I have a drone Pilot's License and I like using it, even if it's just to deliver for dinner."

I sit up. He drapes me in a shimmering wrap he finds among my clothing trays. "This is pretty. Don't want you..."

"Catching cold?"

He nods.

I laugh.

His perceptive words only makes me laugh harder, but have me wincing in pain. "I know, there are far worst things in the universe than a cold. It's silly of me, but hey..."

I smile.

He wraps the warmer gossamer cloth around me.

I rise to set out small golden bowls and matching elegant cups on the lacquered table as it hovers near us. I felt he'd enjoy their beauty. I was right.

He eases to the floor stunned.

"Are those solid gold?"

"Yes. I have much of it here."

The shrimp dumplings and spicy sauce are very good.

As we eat, I notice him trying not to stare at my breast under the wrap.

"When you are not fighting in your armor, do you females always go around naked?"

"Not at all. We enjoy well-crafted dressings but mostly they are weapon and spell proof above all else. Here, there is not a threat to us. Well, that's what I thought. It shall be noted now, Earth has some forms of infestation, sadly."

He sleeps with me in my nest under the stars with the twinkle of city lights below.

The night after, I light the candles on the small table where we dine, then I set out a silken wrap I bought from a merchant in another older age of Earth. I once used it as a wall decoration with its stunning blue skies, pale clouds, dark earthy mountains and soaring golden dragons. It is a thing of immense beauty.

As soon as he sees it draped over one of my suits of armor, he grows quiet.

"Nat, is that a Kimono?" He passes me a bag with a bottle of wine inside.

I feel proud, I've surprised him yet again.

"It is yours. Please, take your things off and be comfortable."

I hear his breath hold. Then in a reverent way, he does as I ask.

I return to my food prepping station dressed in the clean denim shirt he gave me to wear in Central Park.

I chop big green and red peppers with my cleaving knives on the cool side of the large cooking slab. Its chemical reaction to the metal pots I set down on it ignite the bottoms of each pan with the right amount of heat, sensing what I'm cooking.

I feel him approach; he kisses me behind my ear.

"What is that kiss for?"

"This Kimono. It should be in a museum. It's crazy, crazy beautiful."

I don't look at him. I know with his dark skin and greying black hair, he must look stunning.

I know his eyes are sparkling with delight. I will be leaving too soon. Our little time together is growing more painful.

"It is yours when I leave. My cooking may not help you to fly but you will not forget me."

He says, "God, girl, please. Your face is imprinted on my soul."

I make a stew from my stores, loaded with peppers, tomatoes and curry. We eat and drink everything.

He leans away from the small hovering wooden table. As usual, we sit on piles of brightly colored pillows. He leans back.

"Wow. Can I ask, what kinda meat was that?"

I tell him, "Something like your mastodon. They are huge and very good in stew. "

"Mastodon? No shit! That may be why we don't have any left one earth, we must have ate them, 'cause that there was damn good."

He looks fondly at the tub.

"Bath night?"

I nod. "I could use a hot bath, yes."

In moments, it is ready. We sit in the tub in the midst of the space watching steam rise from the water in a luxurious way. We soap our hands together. He laughs, "You used up all my soap and shampoo!"

I shoot him a hard look, "You had so little! I will give you a spellcasted bowel that should never empty. It's a tiny gateway to our supply station for this realm. There are centuries of items stocked there. Try this..."

"Ah, like mango..." He looks at me. "Baby, I'm worried for you."

"Hum, for me? I've never heard those words before."

"What do you mean?"

"What you've said, 'you are worried for me'. I lead troops, Jeremiah. I've killed numberless beings attacking what I hold dear. I've been crippled and broken before. A mate has never said they worry for me. They are concerned but..."

"You always return."

"Yes."

He rolls his eyes. "Hum. Your men take it for granted that you will come home."

He looks at me. "We got plenty of assholes on Earth, way more than we will admit. But I'm really not liking the dudes of your kind, baby."

I shrug, "They are under their own pressures. We accept that. My home worlds are lush and bountiful even after so many eons of war. Our male science sects handle massive defenses for our infrastructure. The devices and strategies are created by our brothers of Science; our defense grid, bombs of gasses, surveillance and weaponized illnesses are mostly from our brother Mystics. The two create defenses for every creature that comes at us, It is astonishing in scope. The average male spellcaster or Tech Specialist has 'mad skills,' as you say. It takes enormous amounts of study for that, and decades of focus. The two males I am mated to, my lot mates — Edel, Master Tech of Russo and Alazar, Dan of the Order of Mystic Commanders — are some of the finest of their craft. They may not be interested in many other aspects of my life but they treat me with care and respect. I have no doubt I'd be missed if I died."

He says, "My bet is you'd be missed more by the troops you serve."

He grumbles, "Edel and Alazar?" He huffs and looks away.

I stay quiet. The tension is forming around him like a dark fog.

"I do not love them."

He looks back at me, surprised.

I study his features.

"I. Do not. Love them. I respect them, we have very good sex. We are to make young together for the good of my kind. I care for them, yes. Nothing more."

I lay my head across his shoulder. Slowly, his good arm wraps around me.

"It will be very hard to leave Earth. I promise you, I will be back here in ten."

"You promise?"

"Only death could stop me."

He helps me from the bath, takes one of my large, thirsty cloths to dry me. I return the favor and dry his strong runner's legs. I find his organ is semi-hard and comfortable. I put my mouth on it. A tremor races through him.

I'm on my knees sucking and licking.

His hand is caressing the back of my neck at the base of my feathered head.

"Let your wings out, I need to see them."

I do. Without stopping my action, my wings ease out and around me.

He gives a soft smile. "Mmm... I keep thinking I'm dreaming."

I stop and smile at him. "This is no dream, sergeant. I plan to exhaust you tonight."

"I'm getting old. It's easy to do these days."

"Quality over quantity, ki?"

"How do you say 'I want to lick you'?"

"Ev sugatan vi maal eva vemaa, I desire to taste your sweetness."

"Vemaa... means sweetness?"

"Ki."

"How do you say my sweetness?"

"Evi vemaa."

He helps me to my feet. He pulls me close and repeats in my ear. "Evi vemaa. That's what you are to me."

His kisses are warm, penetrating, the kind he's realized I like.

His hips indicate his intent to walk. My legs wrap around his waist, his strong arm slides around me and we walk that way to the center of my studio.

He kneels as I slide to his hips. I lay on top of him, my wings outstretched. My warm body feels like it's melting into his. I lay on the plump cushions to one side of him to rub from his chest to his hard cock, my hand moving slow.

His breathing grows faster with arousal.

He says dreamily, "Mmm... Jamaica. My cousin owns a little hotel there. We'd have his best room with our own cove."

"My birth home is in a cliffside cove overlooking the ocean."

"You'll feel at home."

"Is the water blue or clear?" I ask.

"Both. You'll love it. I'll take you when you return here. I will love you up on the beach."

He guides my chin to his mouth. We kiss passionately. I feel his breath grow heavier by the moment, I stroke him, his belly and nuts tighten.

He reaches between my legs and massages my sex; it is already wet.

Still, he licks his fingers and takes my clit in between them to rub.

My eyes close. My hand stroking his organ slows down, my thoughts drift between my legs and the mischievous look on his face.

"You like taunting me there?"

I say. "Yes, I most certainly do."

Concern grows in his eyes. "You were all broken up, bae bae. You ready for some loving?"

I shoot him a stern look. Without words I shift and sit on top of him. His good arm wraps around me as his hips rise, I ease onto his thick, dark shaft.

My fingers slide into his mouth. He sucks them, I tilt over him, my small breasts are in his face. He sucks my nipples and thrusts upwards, cock inside me as I ride him. He reaches up to touch my wings. He strokes and pets the paler downy underside, mesmerized.

I feel a delicious shudder move through me in waves from his delicate caress.

My mouth finds his. From the growing forces in my body, I know I'm reaching the crest of my wave.

He grips a cheek of my ass, halting me from moving.

He's thrusting harder now, his arm keeping me pinned to him.

"Gonna blow..."

I demand, "Together then!"

I squeeze his cock with my sex. He grits his teeth as he tries to resist the last moment. Then, he floods my cup just as I let go.

His back arches, he grips me to him. Cries of pleasure tear from us both.

My levitation lifts us off the ground. I hold him in my arms and with my legs and my sex. I rotate us, he lays draped on top of me a moment. I fold my wings around him. Weightless, we turn slowly, over and over.

My body's responses begin to ease, and we descend to the ground.

He wears a dreamlike smile.

He asks, "Do you believe in God, Nat?"

"If you mean in the sentience of life, a supreme form of creative energy, then yes. Our magical core stems from that. We understand what forces guide us and are grateful to that which binds us to it, to our dead, our worlds and to each other. Why do you ask?"

He traces my cheek.

"Cause every second I'm with you, I'm thanking my higher power for knowing you, woman. I thank God you chose to be with this old war dog with a busted limb."

We lower to the piles of soft old rugs below.

I whisper, "Sometimes, you say things that get me where I live, Jeremiah, you get me in the quiet parts of my being."

"Mmm..."

We lay in a pool of moonlight.

We fall fast asleep.

{10}

Our last precious days are spent on long walks around the city's even quieter Greenwich Village area, near the river that almost claimed my life. We meander in Central Park and hit small charming bars and cafes to listen to musicians play.

A few times I hear him mumble something like, "Edel, Alazar, hum. Fuckers. Better do right by my female."

I didn't bring their names up again, yet his anger simmers. It is night time. We exit a ridiculously tiny space aptly named, "Smalls." Its musicians were some of the best I've heard on Earth so far. Leaving late, we step over people sitting on the steps, listening in.

I've seen hints of his jealousy for hours. I ask him as we walk a quiet tree lined street, "Are you well?"

"Yes. Why?"

"I heard you, you sound a little upset."

He shakes his head. "I'm just not liking the thought of you returning home to a pair of selfish brilliant, good-looking winged pricks."

I sigh. "Oh, them. You are being too..."

"Salty?" He finishes.

I consider the tight and sharp taste of the mineral.

I conclude, "Yes! A good choice. You are being too salty about my lot mates, my man. I can't change the system I was born under. It works well under the strange circumstances we exist under, but I am not a victim of it. I choose to be with you even if it is off-world."

He stops walking. "But you are not allowed to stay on Earth if you want, and bad shit would happen to you if we are found out."

"My duty is to my cluster and my kind. I will serve that duty until I am no longer useful. I will abide by the rules. Still, I have some choices in my life. Being with you in my off time is my choice. This keeps me from being victimized by the system I live under. You have a much shorter lifespan than I. I am mindful of every moment I have here with you. I'll have all this locked in my mind, my heart. Understand, I don't want to be exiled and lose everything I've gained in my life but to keep this memory I would face that, if it came to it."

I grab his good arm. He stops walking, turns to face me.

"I care for my lot mates, sergeant but I'd not willingly face exile for them."

I see him process what I've said. He takes up my hand and kisses it.

"Grandam."

We walk the quiet tree lined streets of Greenwich again, enjoying each other's company.

Our last night is a Friday.

We meet and walk downtown. I wear the silky red dress.

"Mmm... Can you leave that one with me?"

"A strange request; you cannot fit into it."

He laughs his eyes are bright like a child's.

"No! No, I won't wear it. I want to remember you this night, silly!"

He kisses me.

An old bald black man in ruined clothes eases past us.

"'Scuse me, lovebirds."

We break our kiss, as battle tension races through us. We stare at the man, checking him over for eyestalks or anything out of the ordinary.

The old male says, "You better show that queen a good night, my brother!"

Jeremiah laughs and shakes his head. "Will do. Ah, my city..."

A few feet away, we stop walking. He points to a wide stone staircase that climbs to a grand, glowing plaza and cream-colored elegant buildings before us. The light all about the place is dreamlike and golden.

"This is Lincoln Center. They give events inside and outside. People flow in here to be entertained but I like to stop buy randomly. This is where I met my boy the horny conga player."

We walk up the stairs. I watch the casual flow of people walking and admiring the cool night air. I say, "I'd never be attracted to him. He entertains very well, he is attractive but he's not about anyone but himself."

My mate laughs.

"Yeah, he's mad fun and a good friend but he'd throw his momma under a bus for whatever he needed. How did you know?"

I give him a sidelong glance, "How do you know if a soldier may possess the core needed for a mission?"

He looks at me, he takes my hand. "I take it you can assess a fighter or flyer with how well she performs her common duties under stress. You have to, right?"

"Right."

He gives me a sly look, "What do you think of me?"

"It is not good to say. You might try to tamper with yourself."

"What? Tamper..."

"Yes, I care for you the way you are. I'd not want you to try to work on something that needs no improvements."

"Mmm... do you think I would do that? Really?"

"I did not say that you would. It's best not to dangle it at you though. What is that sound? More music?"

I am standing, but my hips are swaying in a rhythmic way.

He asks, "Do you like it? Your hips like it."

He takes my hand and we start dancing, he draws me into the largest crowd of dancers I've seen on this trip to Earth. I stop.

I've been lucky: I've not been clumsy and broken anything, except the plug of our first wine.

"What is it baby, you afraid?"

I glance at him, "To dance in a crowd? No, I love dancing. I love dancing with you."

He beams and places his palm against my face in a tender way. I help put his damaged arm around me. We glide into the dancing crowd.

Everything is easy and beautiful as always.

Until, I step on his foot.

"Shit!"

I stop again.

"We should stop..."

"No. You are exciting in that dress, your power is shining through. I know how much you love to dance."

"That is very, very beautiful but our last night will not end well if I break your foot."

He smirks, "You mean you are clumsy and dangerous? Well... Did you ever injure your babies?"

I freeze. I drop his hands and step away from him. The thought of that kills the mood. I turn to leave.

"Nat!"

I move at just above a human speed. I'm appalled and angry.

"Nat! Please!"

I whirl around.

I hiss, "Why would you ask such nonsense? If my hand hurt my fledglings I'd cut it off and burn it myself!"

He's close to me. "I believe you. If you didn't hurt your babies, you'd not hurt me. Unless you don't care for me."

I'm frozen. "I... I..."

I see his line of thinking.

I say, "I am sorry. The thought of hurting my young... Yes, even now I know I'll leave tomorrow evening but I would die to protect you."

He eases his arm around me. We are one again. We stand on the Grand Concourse of the elegant open plaza. People in fine dress pass us by. We embrace and the world grows quiet, time stands still. When we move again, he guides me to the park across town.

"Is this still... Central Park?"

"Yes." he says.

"Ah. It is wonderful. Too bad it does not float above the city. It could be reconstructed, bi-level or even more."

"You have that kind of thing at home?"

"Yes. Many structures float. Cities, mountains, citadels... I've told you of our technologies and spellcasting before I am certain. My talk about floating cities must be strange for you."

"I love it, all of it."

He looks at me. He kisses the back of our clasped hands. The park is lit at dusk. Few couples and joggers pass us by as we wander down paths and street lamps.

He stops me. "Nat..."

"Yes?"

"These men, the human men on your world... They please their mates?"

"I've heard as much. They must, in every way I suppose. They were fought for. They would have been eradicated."

"Your elite class would have killed them if they could?"

"Yes. They are men outside of time from your world and could not be returned in the numbers they'd grown to. We had thousands and thousands of Earthmen. There are legends of angels and winged beings taking them to some reward after death for a reason. After being with us they absorb too many of our secrets."

He nods.

I continue, "The Golgorn. They are their own small army of lovers. Armies have been known to destroy those that rule over them. They can be dangerous."

He nods. "The Romans and others knew that. Armies have overthrown governments time and time again. Man, an army of lovers? They must be pretty damn scary. If I was one of these men... I'd kill anything or anybody that threatened your pretty feathered head."

He stops walking and touches my cheeks. I wear a red satin head wrapping. He eases it back enough to see the feathers of my head peek through.

He looks into my eyes.

"I don't enjoy killing. To protect you? I'd be a fucking butcher."

"I. Know."

Soon, we stand in the shadow of the Church. I wrap my arms around him and push up hard. We are at my nest in seconds.

There are no words between us. I feel the sadness of loss threatening my mind already. It will be only months for me but still there are no guarantees in my life aside from another skirmish, another full-out war with some group desperately wanting what we have. Death happens.

When I return, his hair will be grayer. He may have a few deeper lines were he smiles. I will welcome them, I will grab him and kiss those lines and massage his older body as I'm sure he will do for me.

We start undressing the moment we reach my nest. I strip away his leather jacket. His belt is next, then his pants and soft shirt. Tonight he wore no undergarment: his cock stands tall as if asking for the firm grip of my mouth and cunt. He bites my nipples hard with my dress still on, hard enough for me to yelp. They are the only really sensitive part of my battle-worn body, outside of my sex.

We both shove the dress from my form. We are naked under the chill of the night. I wrap him up and we fall into the feathered down. This will be our very last intimate moment.

We go at it with a newfound intensity.

We try to brand the moment into our flesh as if we'd not already made a ton of memories this trip.

He growls, "My sweetness! Mine, Goddamn it!"

He flips me face down. He takes me from behind. He leans close to my earlobe, biting it. In a husky voice he calls me. "Nat! I won't come easy, baby. Not tonight!"

I tell him, "We shall see. I enjoy making you holler!"

In moments, there is only movement, sweat and heavy breathing. There is no talk about his age; there is little talk at all. We are warriors and lovers and we will soon be parted.

Hours later, we stand on his balcony, molded in an embrace. He wears the stunning Kimono I'd gifted to him. I am naked as the day we met. We've showered in the endless enchanted cleansers and soaps I'd given him in a large basket made of precious gold carved with spells both inside and out. Their delicious fragrance wafts around us.

He breathes in my scent before he speaks. He trembles, his cheeks are wet with tears.

"How will you get home?"

"A wall in my compound is false. With the right spells, it is a portal."

He shakes his head, a stern shrouds his face. "Don't you forget. Swear to me."

"I swear."

"Cross your heart and hope to die. Say it."

"I... cross my heart. This is a curse?"

"Yes. It's a childish curse."

"I see that you understand that even childish curses have power. I hope to die if I do not meet you in ten years."

We hold each other until I can no longer deny the pull of my gut. My time on Earth is over. The link to my sister-fighters grows impossible to deny. My energy-body is fluttering inside me to unite with the magic of my realm; I'm shaking from this as I ease from his arms.

I study his sad face.

He whispers, "Goodbye, baby."

I lift into the air. Naked, I hover above him like I did weeks ago. The pull is starting to feel like agony on my insides, but still I hold off. I study him.

"There are no goodbyes for us."

He smile almost reaches his eyes. "Ki ute."

I float upwards, his eyes locked to mine. "Yes, yes indeed."

I take off to my nest, allowing the pull to draw me back. Closer to the gate, the summoning on me eases within my keep.

My movements are mechanical. I don my armor, wrap the last of my gear in my travel pack.

I do my usual three sweeps, dousing all the light orbs, falling hard into the formality of cleansing and protection spells.

In an hour, Earth's time, I'm at the portal gate. It irises open in a section of stone wall I've been through hundreds of times. It reveals a cavernous landscape, with a dazzling array of stars above and a deceptively simple endless rock pathway.

My armor on, I am ready.

Before him, I looked forward to returning home. Even now, I miss my fledglings, Blue Squadron, Emera Cluster, Temple Tosca and everything about my worlds.

Still, I am tortured. I feel shattered.

I hiss, "Suca, umkaha. Hassa. This sucks. This so sucks, damn it."

I fall to my knees, sobbing.

I quiet down, eventually. Shaking, I rise.

I look over my shoulder past the darkened room, at my weatherized nest.

I know he's watching. I take up one of the ornate holders and whisper a spell to light it's tapered candlestick, one that once lit our dinners. I walk to my nest and stand on its edge.

He sees me and waves with his good hand. He kisses his palm and blows at me.

Even in my pain, I am happy for one last moment with him.

The pull of my mystical ties to my worlds, my fighters, fledglings and my duty, will not be denied any longer. I am shaking violently. I wave and ease inside.

I blow out the candle and place it on the floor in front of the gate. I take up my pack, put one foot in front of the other onto the path. The Earth gate closes behind me. I follow the mystical call of my people: it begs me to fly.

In tears, I walk the path for as long as I can.

TO BE CONTINUED...

Afterword

Thank you for reading Under Naked Skies! If you enjoyed this book, please leave a quick review on Amazon!

Book three of Kiss the Sky, Departure of Love, will be released January 2018. To pre-order, leave a request for the author at Nigia@nigiastephens.com

About the Author

Nigia has read her prose and short stories in the New York City area since 1989. Her writing explores, alternative fiction, erotica and myriad forms of fantasy. She recently published the short story, Kiss the Sky now available on Amazon. Under Naked Skies is book two of the series.

Her debut novel, A Time of Blood and Fire, will be re-released as three-part series in 2017. More of her upcoming releases are listed below.

She was spotlighted as a new talent for her short story, The Love of Dangerous Creatures, at http://BookCountry.com. Read it at http://blog.bookcountry.com/member-spotlight-meet-writer-nigia-stephens/ Nigia posts new writing and musings on her site, Nigiastephens.com and on Facebook as Nigiawriter.

Explore the site, http://www.NigiaStephens.com for more info on upcoming arts, events and readings!

2017, 2018 Releases

Under Naked Skies

Departure of Love

The Love of Dangerous Creatures

Arms of Angels,

Cauldrons of War

based on A Time of Blood and Fire

Dark Desires

www.ingramcontent.com/pod-product-compliance
Lightning Source LLC
Chambersburg PA
CBHW071340130626
46556CB00004B/1960